PUPPY PATROL ™

TRICK OR TREAT?

BOOKS IN THE PUPPY PATROL SERIES ™

PUPPY PATROL ™

TRICK OR TREAT?

JENNY DALE

Illustrations by Mick Reid
Cover illustration by Michael Rowe

AN
APPLE
PAPERBACK

SCHOLASTIC INC.
New York Toronto London Auckland Sydney
Mexico City New Delhi Hong Kong Buenos Aires

**TO ENDAL, DOG OF THE MILLENNIUM
SPECIAL THANKS TO ANDREA ABBOTT**

No part of this publication may be reproduced, in whole or in part, or stored in
a retrieval system, or transmitted in any form or by any means, electronic,
mechanical, photocopying, recording, or otherwise, without the written
permission of the publisher. For information regarding permission,
please write to Macmillan Publishers Ltd., 20 New Wharf Rd.,
London N1 9RR Basingstoke and Oxford.

ISBN 0-439-54362-2

Copyright © 2001 by Working Partners Limited.
Illustrations copyright © 2001 by Mick Reid.

All rights reserved. Published by Scholastic Inc., 557 Broadway,
New York, NY 10012, by arrangement with Macmillan Children's Books,
a division of Macmillan Publishers Ltd.

SCHOLASTIC and associated logos are trademarks and/or registered trademarks
of Scholastic Inc.

12 11 10 9 8 7 6 5 4 3 2   3 4 5 6 7 8/0

Printed in the U.S.A.
First Scholastic printing, October 2003

"There! All done," Neil Parker announced. He put down his paintbrush and held up a black sweatshirt on which he'd painted the long white ribs and bones of a skeleton. "What do you think of this, Jake?"

Hearing his name, the young Border collie sprang up from the floor and wagged his tail eagerly.

Neil laughed and patted Jake's head. "No, we're not going for a walk." He looked outside. It was dark and raining heavily. "Besides, you wouldn't want to be out there right now."

Neil's sister, Emily, stapled a cardboard brim to the base of her witch's hat. "How does this look?" she asked, putting it on. She hunched her shoulders and cackled like a witch.

1

Neil burst out laughing. "You sound like you're in pain."

Jake shot Emily a quick look, then settled down calmly again at Neil's feet.

"So much for your scary Halloween costume," Neil added. "Jake didn't even bat an eyelid."

"Well, I haven't finished it yet," said Emily, taking off the hat.

"My witch's cloak is very scary," piped up Sarah, their five-year-old sister. "My friend said so. Didn't you?" She turned away, draping a piece of black cloth over her shoulders.

"What friend?" Emily asked. She glanced around the kitchen. Other than the three of them and Jake, there was no one there.

"This friend, here," said Sarah, solemnly pointing to the chair beside her. "I'm going to make her a ghost costume for when we go out trick-or-treating on Friday."

Neil grinned. "Great idea. It should really suit her."

"What should suit who?" asked Carole Parker, coming into the kitchen from the office.

"A ghost costume for Sarah's imaginary friend," Emily told her mother with a smile.

"Oh, I see," said Carole, winking at Emily. Then, turning to Neil, she said, "That was Mrs. McArthur on the phone. She wanted to make sure her dog didn't miss her too much."

"But she called yesterday and I told her that Major

was fine," Neil said, shaking his head. "Didn't she believe me?"

"She probably did," said Emily, rolling up a sheet of unused cardboard. "But it sounds like she's the one who's lonely — not Major!"

Carole laughed. "Better that way. Bev's had her hands full as it is. I don't know how she would have coped with a miserable Toy Pomeranian!"

Neil's family ran King Street Kennels just outside the country town of Compton. The kennel was always full this time of year, when many people went on vacation. Bev Mitchell, one of the full-time kennel assistants was working round-the-clock, while the other kennel assistant, Kate Paget, was out on maternity leave because she was going to have a baby.

"I don't know what we would have done without Bev this week," Carole went on. "She's worked harder than ever. And, of course," she smiled at Neil and Emily, "you've both been a big help, too."

Neil had been only too eager to help as much as he could. As far as he was concerned, working with dogs was no chore at all. In fact, that's exactly what he wanted to do when he finished school, because dogs were more important to him than anything.

Carole turned to Sarah. "Now, young lady — bathtime for you."

"But it's still early," Sarah complained. "It's not usually dark at this time."

"Yes, but you're all back at school tomorrow," Carole replied. "Vacation's over now." She went toward the door. "Come on."

Sarah tried another tactic. "But I haven't finished making my costume yet."

"Maybe your secret friend can do it for you, Squirt," Neil grinned.

Sarah made a face at her brother. "She doesn't know how to," she muttered, then stomped out of the kitchen behind her mother.

Neil put away the paint and brush and hung his sweatshirt over the back of a chair to dry. Then he picked up a magazine on dogs and turned to an article on Basenjis. He was so absorbed in reading about the African barkless dog that he didn't hear a car pulling up outside.

Jake, who certainly knew how to use his voice, started barking enthusiastically.

"That must be Dad," said Emily. She glanced at her watch. "He's home early."

Bob Parker had gone to a talk at the steam train club with his friend Jim Brewster, the local train signalman. Jim owned Skip, Jake's uncle. Bob was passionate about trains — almost as much as he was about dogs.

Jake looked appealingly at Neil, then began to scratch at the door to the hall, whining to be let out.

"It's only Dad, Jake," said Neil, glancing up from the magazine. He patted his leg. "Here, boy. Lie down now."

Jake crouched at the door, sniffing through the

gap at the bottom. Neil wondered for a moment why Jake was more excited than usual to hear Bob coming home, but he turned his attention back to the magazine article. He hadn't even read another sentence when there came a loud knocking on the front door.

"So it isn't Dad!" said Neil, getting up and going to see who it was.

A tall, slim woman Neil had never seen before was waiting on the porch. Next to her stood an elegant, silver-gray Standard poodle.

With a delighted yap, Jake squeezed past Neil

and began sniffing the newcomer. The poodle briefly touched Jake's nose in a friendly greeting, then sat down and looked alertly around her.

"Hello," said Neil in surprise. He was sure they weren't expecting any more boarders that evening. He smiled at the dog, who gazed back at him with an interested expression on her intelligent face. "Can I help you?" he asked the woman politely. "Is your dog going to be staying with us?"

"Yes — if that's possible," the stranger replied, pushing her short gray hair off her forehead. "I'm afraid it's very important that she does."

The woman seemed very anxious and Neil wondered if something was wrong. "Please come inside," he said. "I'll call my mom for you."

"I *do* hope you can accommodate Sapphire," said the woman, following Neil through the hall and into the kitchen. The poodle walked obediently next to her while Jake bounded ahead. "You see, my daughter was injured in an accident this afternoon and has been taken to the hospital. She has children of her own, and I need to go up to Cumbria right away to take care of them."

Neil saw that the woman was close to tears. He pulled out a chair for her. "Would you like to sit down while I get I my mom?" he said.

Instantly, the poodle sat on the floor next to the chair.

"I don't think Neil was talking to you!" Emily

chuckled, patting the dog's silver head. "I'll go upstairs and get Mom," she said, and hurried out.

The woman sat anxiously on the edge of the chair,
twisting the leash in her hands. In contrast, Sapphire
waited quietly at her side. Neil was impressed by how
calm the dog was. He wondered why the woman would
need to leave her behind. The poodle seemed so well
behaved he was sure she could be taken anywhere.
"Can't you take Sapphire with you?" he asked.

"I'm afraid not," said the woman, standing up and
going over to the window. "You see, she isn't mine
and I really can't take her away. I'm looking after her
for a good friend." She turned and held out a folder
that contained some documents. "I have all her
vaccination papers and her license with me, if you
need them. And she's been fed this evening, so you
won't have to worry about that."

Neil took the papers from her just as Carole and
Emily came into the kitchen.

"Hello," said Carole. "Emily tells me you need to
leave your dog with us."

"I'm very sorry to trouble you on a Sunday evening,"
said the woman, turning to Carole. She clasped her
hands anxiously to her chest, dropping Sapphire's
leash as she did so. Feeling the leash slacken, the
poodle picked it up in her mouth and walked around
the room with her tail wagging, greeting each of the
Parkers in turn.

"My name's Hilary Herson and this is my friend's

dog," the woman explained. "Kevin Dunbar, Sapphire's owner, is also in the hospital, so it's an awkward situation. I would never think of leaving Sapphire under ordinary circumstances, but I don't really have a choice — and I've heard such good reports about King Street Kennels," she finished.

Carole smiled. "Thank you. Of course Sapphire is very welcome to stay with us," she went on, "but since we're bursting at the seams at the moment . . ."

Mrs. Herson's face dropped. "Oh dear," she began.

"No, it isn't a problem," Carole said quickly. "I was about to say that the boarding section is full, but there is some room in the rescue center."

In addition to running the boarding kennel, the Parkers also took in lost or abandoned dogs until their owners came to claim them or new homes could be found. "If you don't mind," said Carole, "we can keep her there for the time being."

"I'm sure that will be fine," said Mrs. Herson, "as long as Sapphire has her own pen."

"Of course," Carole assured her.

While Carole took down Mrs. Herson's contact information and checked Sapphire's vaccination certificates, Neil and Emily made a fuss over the poodle, who responded by gently licking their hands.

"She's so friendly," Emily observed, stroking Sapphire's velvety ears.

"And really relaxed," Neil added. He took the neatly

trimmed paw that Sapphire was offering him and shook it with pretend seriousness.

"Yes, you won't have to worry about settling her in," said Mrs. Herson. She glanced out the window again. "I really have to go," she said. "This rain will make the journey even slower." She bent down and gave Sapphire a good-bye hug, then hurried over to the door, saying, "I'll call you from Cumbria, Mrs. Parker, just to make sure everything's all right." And with that, she was gone.

"Well, that was quite a surprise," said Carole. She slipped the documents back into the folder. "Please take Sapphire to the rescue center, Neil. And Emily, would you file these papers away for me?"

Neil picked up the leash. Sapphire was standing with her head to one side, looking at the door and listening to Mrs. Herson drive away. Then she turned attentively toward Neil. "Come and see your new home," said Neil. He stepped forward and the poodle began to walk next to him, perfectly matching his pace.

Neil was impressed. "She's well trained," he said, going over to the back door. "Come on, Jake. You can come, too."

Delighted to be going out, the Border collie shot through the door and darted across the courtyard, splashing through the puddles outside the kennel block. Sapphire trotted delicately next to Neil, lifting her paws high as if she didn't want to get them wet.

By the time they reached the rescue section, the Border collie was soaked. "What am I going to do with you, you silly dog?" Neil laughed, opening the door.

They went inside and Sapphire looked around inquisitively. A bright overhead light lit up the central section of the circular building, making the other dogs sit up and blink at the visitors.

In the first pen was a brown-and-white Jack Russell called Sailor who had been found roaming beside the river the day before. He was wearing a collar that had his name on it but no address or telephone number. Bob Parker had given the dog's description to Sergeant Moorhead and Terri McCall at

the SPCA, but if no one claimed Sailor in a month, then a new home would be found for him. As soon as he saw them, Sailor ran to the gate and stood up against it, whining excitedly.

Jake rushed over to him, swishing his tail from side to side. Sapphire was also eager to meet the little terrier. She strained against her leash and pushed her black nose against the wire, sniffing curiously.

Jake then bounded along to the dog in the next pen — a handsome Rottweiler called Nina who had been found in the fields two days ago. Unlike the Jack Russell, the tag on her collar listed both her name and address, which meant that the Parkers had been able to trace her owners very quickly. Nina was scheduled to be picked up the following afternoon.

The third dog was an enormous young bullmastiff called Titus whose owner could no longer keep him because she had to move into a small apartment. Sapphire seemed undaunted by the size and strength of the big brown dog and greeted him cheerfully through the wire. In return, Titus dropped to his belly and looked up playfully at the poodle, his short, stubby tail wagging rapidly.

"I'm glad you like him, Sapphire," said Neil, "because he's going to be your neighbor." He opened the gate to pen number four next door, wondering if Sapphire would hesitate like some dogs did when being led into a strange place. "Come on, Sapphire, time for bed," he said.

Sapphire looked up at him, then stepped into the pen. Neil waited while she inspected her new surroundings, then he closed the gate and went to fetch her a bowl of water and a handful of dog biscuits.

When he came back, Sapphire was lying down in the bed at the back of the pen. She jumped up as soon as she saw Neil and padded over to the wire. Neil dropped the biscuits onto the floor of the pen and Sapphire crunched them up happily.

Outside the pen, Jake barked sharply. "All right," said Neil with a grin, throwing him a biscuit. "Here's one for you, too." He took one last look at the other dogs, who were settling down in their beds again, and flicked off the light. Then he pulled up his hood and stepped back out into the rain.

Neil watched Jake streaking ahead through the puddles. He ran to catch up with him. "It would be nice if you picked up some of Sapphire's good manners," he said, laughing.

Jake looked up at him, his mouth wide open as if he were laughing back at Neil. Then he shook himself vigorously, sending a spray of water all over Neil, before charging off again.

"See what I mean!" Neil spluttered, chasing Jake toward the back door.

CHAPTER TWO

Neil was toweling Jake dry in the utility room when there was another knock at the door.

"I'll get it," said Emily. "Maybe it's Mrs. Herson again."

Carole looked up from the dog magazine she was reading. "I wonder if she changed her mind about leaving Sapphire here?" she said.

Neil left Jake lapping water from his bowl in the utility room and peered down the hall to see. But it wasn't Mrs. Herson. Instead, two more people stood on the unlit porch — a girl about Neil's age and a short, stocky man wearing glasses. Emily showed them in, and as they came into the kitchen Neil realized that the girl was cradling a small, coppery-gold puppy in her arms.

Another boarder, Neil thought, putting down Jake's towel. *If things keep up like this, I'll have to give up my bedroom soon!* He smiled to himself as he went over to meet the tiny stranger.

Jake charged across to greet the puppy, too, but Neil managed to grab him. "Down, boy," he said. The collie obediently dropped to the floor and lay there with his head between his front paws, his eyes darting from side to side as he sized up the new arrivals.

"Can we help you?" Carole asked.

"I hope so," said the man. "You're Mrs. Parker, aren't you?"

Carole nodded.

"I'm Martin O'Donnell and this is my daughter Helen," he said. He pointed to the puppy. "We found this little fellow earlier and we're hoping you'll be able to take him in."

"Found him? Where?" Neil asked, astonished that such a young puppy would have been wandering around on his own. Neil thought he looked less than three months old.

"On the road to Colshaw," said Helen, her blue eyes wide with concern. "He looked lost and was running all over the road." Protectively, she drew him closer to her. "It's lucky he wasn't hit by a car."

The little dog glanced up at Helen, then looked around at the others. Settling his gaze on Neil, he thumped his little tail against Helen's chest and whined softly.

"We picked him up and took him home. Then we called the police," Mr. O'Donnell explained. "But Sergeant Moorhead said they'd had no reports of any missing dogs. He suggested we bring him here. He said you have a rescue center and that you might even know who he belongs to."

Carole put out her hand for the puppy to sniff. "We usually hear about litters of puppies born in Compton," she said. "But I don't recognize him. Do you?" she asked, turning to Neil and Emily.

Neil stroked the puppy, who licked his hand eagerly with his rough, pink tongue. "No, I've never seen him before," he said.

Emily shook her head. "Me neither."

"Well, it looks like we have another visitor," said Carole, holding out her arms toward the puppy.

Helen hesitated for a moment, then handed him to Carole. The little dog wriggled with delight as he found himself transferred to another friendly person. "Aren't you a cute little fellow!" Carole exclaimed. She ran her hand over the puppy's side, then put him on the floor and watched him closely.

The puppy sniffed around for a moment. As soon as he spotted Neil crouched down on the floor nearby, he scampered gleefully over to him.

"He's sort of thin, isn't he?" Neil commented. He scooped him up in his arms, feeling the puppy's ribs just under his skin.

"Mmm," said Carole. She bent down next to Neil and looked inside the little dog's mouth and ears and checked his eyes. The puppy lay calmly in Neil's arms, allowing Carole to examine him. "He seems to be in reasonable health," Carole said when she'd finished checking him over. "Just a little thin for his age — which is probably about ten weeks. But Mike will be here in the morning, so he can take a good look at him and vaccinate him at the same time, just in case he hasn't had his shots yet."

Mike Turner was the Compton vet. He was coming to King Street for his weekly checkup of the boarders and rescue dogs.

"He was really starving," said Helen, kneeling down next to Neil. "So we bought him some puppy food on the way home. You should have seen how he gobbled it up."

Seeing a familiar face, the puppy twisted his way out of Neil's arms, then climbed onto Helen's lap and began chewing one of the wooden toggles on her coat.

"No, you can't eat that, Trick!" Helen chuckled, gently prying the toggle out of the puppy's mouth.

"Trick?" Emily echoed. "Is that his name?"

Helen nodded. "Well, it's what I called him," she explained shyly. "I thought of Trick because it's Halloween. But I know he probably has a name already." She caressed the puppy's soft, fluffy ears.

"It's more likely that he *doesn't* have a name already," said Neil solemnly.

The others looked at him. "What do you mean?" Emily asked.

Neil shrugged. "Oh, just that he's so young, he might not have been given a name yet," he said, although privately he had begun to suspect that someone may have abandoned the puppy. Why else would he be so thin? There was no sign of a collar, either — not even flattened fur around the puppy's neck, which would suggest that a collar had fallen off.

Neil sighed deeply. It was bad enough that people dumped animals they didn't want — but to do it to such a young dog was even more outrageous. And such a beautiful puppy, too! He ran his hand across Trick's fluffy, golden coat, then gazed at his gentle face. The puppy stared back at him with an intelligent, friendly expression that reminded Neil strongly of Labradors and retrievers. "He's a bit of a mix, but I think he's mainly golden retriever," Neil said out loud.

"I think so, too," his mom agreed. "Look how his coat is already getting wavy."

Meanwhile, unable to keep still any longer, Jake was squirming forward on his belly. Soon he was almost in Helen's lap, too. With his thick tail thudding on the floor, he nosed the younger dog, who was stretching up on his hind legs and licking Helen's neck.

Helen laughed with delight. The puppy stretched up even farther and sniffed her long hair before sliding back down to her lap and flipping over on his back

while Jake sniffed him all over. Trick lay perfectly still for a few moments before he decided that it was time to play. He rolled over and clambered off Helen's lap, then bounced around Jake, yapping softly.

"It looks like he'll have no trouble settling in here," Mr. O'Donnell observed. He put his hand on Helen's shoulder. "We should be on our way now, honey."

"Before you go," said Carole quickly, "I need to take down your contact information. Just a formality, really."

Mr. O'Donnell told her their telephone number and address.

"I know that house," said Carole, writing the information on a piece of paper. "It's been empty for a while."

"That's right," Mr. O'Donnell replied. "We moved in two weeks ago. I've been transferred to Compton from Eindhoven in Holland."

"You don't sound Dutch," said Emily.

Mr. O'Donnell laughed. "No, we're not. You see, I work for a computer software company, and my job takes us to lots of different countries. We've almost lost count of the number of places we've lived in so far."

"That must be really cool," Emily said to Helen, who was still kneeling on the floor.

Helen shrugged and flicked her hair behind her shoulders. "It's OK, except that, when we live abroad, I have to go to boarding school. It also means that we can't have any pets," she said, stroking the puppy who was climbing onto her lap again.

"Why not?" asked Neil. He reached over and ruffled Jake's ears. He couldn't imagine being without animals, especially dogs!

"Well, when my mom was a little girl, her family moved abroad with their dog," Helen explained. "And when they came back to England, they had to put him in quarantine for six months. She said it was horrible and she'd never do that to a pet again."

Neil agreed. "It's all right leaving them somewhere for a short time when you go on vacation or something. But six months must be awful!"

"Will you be going to boarding school while you're in Compton?" Emily asked.

Helen's face lit up. "No. That's the great thing about coming here. It's for a whole year, so I'll be living at home and going to school in Compton."

"That's great!" said Neil. "I wonder if you'll be in my class?"

While they were talking, the puppy had grown sleepy. He snuggled inside Helen's jacket, curled up tightly, and was soon fast asleep.

Mr. O'Donnell turned to leave. "Come on, Helen," he said. "We'd really better get going now."

Helen looked pleadingly at her father. "But Trick's sleeping. I don't want to disturb him."

"Don't worry," said Carole kindly. "He won't mind.

And anyway, he'll go right back to sleep as soon as he's settled in the rescue center."

Helen started to say something, but it was clear that she was pretty upset. She swallowed, then stood up slowly, trying not to wake the puppy.

"I'll tell you what," Carole suggested. "Why don't you go with Neil and Emily to settle him in his pen, and I'll make your dad a cup of tea."

"Great!" said Helen at once. She glanced at her father, who smiled and shrugged his shoulders. Then she pulled her jacket closer around the sleeping puppy and followed Neil and Emily out into the courtyard.

Inside the rescue block, Neil opened the gate to the empty pen next to Sapphire. The poodle seemed pleased to see him again. She stood up and came over to the fence, wagging her short tail. Neil pushed his fingers through the wire and scratched the top of her woolly head.

Helen carefully put the puppy down on the soft bedding inside the plastic dog basket. As soon as Trick felt her arms being removed from him, his eyes shot open. He shook his head once or twice, then glanced around to see where he was.

His eyes opened very wide when he spotted the big poodle next door. At once, Trick jumped up and scurried over to the wire partition between them. Sapphire lay down on her belly and sniffed the little puppy through the fence. Trick touched noses with her and then, through the small gap in the wire, tried to lick the sides of her mouth in a gesture of friendly submission.

"He's made a friend," Helen said happily. She turned to Neil. "How long does it usually take to find a home for a stray puppy?"

"It varies from dog to dog," Neil told her. "But a terrific puppy like him won't be here for long. He'll have a new home before you know it."

"Do you really think so?" Helen asked anxiously.

Neil nodded. "Most people would love to have a puppy like Trick. And as soon as he looks settled, we'll go back to the house and check with the police again in case someone's been looking for him. Then we'll phone the SPCA to let them know we have a stray."

"We also have a web site," Emily added. "We'll put all his info on there."

Helen seemed relieved. "It sounds like he'll be famous in no time at all," she said with a smile. "So someone is bound to recognize him."

"That's if anyone is actually looking for him," Neil muttered.

Emily frowned at her brother. "What do you mean?"

Neil squatted down and tapped the wire to draw Trick's attention. "I've got a feeling that he's probably been abandoned," he said, sighing heavily.

Helen looked horrified. "But who would do that to such a tiny, helpless pup?" she cried.

For a moment no one said anything. Trick trotted over and licked Neil's fingers, then, spying the blanket in his basket, ran over and began tussling with it.

Neil stood up and, with another sigh, answered Helen's question. "Someone who just doesn't like dogs as much as we do."

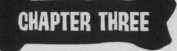

CHAPTER THREE

"**S**ee you later," Neil called to Emily as she left him outside the bicycle shed and went to join her friends in the playground at Meadowbank School the next morning.

"No, you won't," Emily called back. "I've got soccer practice after school," she reminded him.

Neil swung his backpack over his shoulder and was heading toward his friends when he spotted Helen coming through the gate. He waved to her.

Helen ran over to him. "I'm so glad to see you," she said. Then, almost in the same breath, she asked, "How's Trick?"

"He's great," said Neil. "Eating like there's no tomorrow."

"Typical retriever." Helen grinned. "Always greedy!"

"Are you talking about me?" came a voice behind them.

"No way!" Neil laughed, recognizing the voice of his friend, Hasheem Lindon. "Trick's nowhere near as greedy as you!" He turned to Helen. "This is Hasheem — the class clown."

Hasheem smiled at Helen. "Hi," he said. "You're new, aren't you?"

"Yes. I'm Helen O'Donnell," she told him.

"And who's Trick?" Hasheem asked.

"A gorgeous golden retriever cross puppy," Helen said quickly.

"Is he yours?" asked Hasheem.

"I wish!" Helen exclaimed, glancing at Neil. She shook her head. "No. He's a stray that my dad and I found last night. We took him to King Street Kennels."

"So if he's a stray and you like him so much, why don't you keep him?" suggested Hasheem.

Helen shrugged and slung her bag over her shoulder. Neil noticed that it was covered with lots of stickers of different breeds of dogs. Helen explained briefly about her father's work, and how all the traveling meant they couldn't have a pet.

"That's a shame," said Hasheem when she had finished, "because you're obviously crazy about dogs." He glanced at Neil and grinned. "But probably not as crazy as Neil is! He'd go nuts if he wasn't surrounded by dogs day and night."

Neil laughed. He was used to his friends teasing

him about his love of dogs. "But don't tell me you're not crazy about Bessie! You even carry her picture around with you."

"Who's Bessie?" Helen asked.

"My springer spaniel," said Hasheem, instantly producing a photograph of a tan-and-white spaniel from his bag.

Just then the bell rang. "Oh well, back to the grind," said Hasheem. "Whose class are you in, Helen?"

"Mrs. Sharpe's," Helen replied.

"Great!" said Neil. "She's our class teacher, too."

Helen's eyes lit up. "That means I'll definitely see you every day and you can tell me all about Trick," she said happily.

"I don't think you should just *hear* about him,"

said Neil. "Why don't you come over this evening to visit him?"

"I'd love that," Helen exclaimed, beaming with pleasure.

"And you can help me take a picture of him for our web site," Neil added. "He can be our dog of the week on the rescue center's home page."

A deafening clamor of barking and whining reached Neil and Helen as they walked across the courtyard to the kennel block early that evening.

"I think if I was blindfolded, I could still find my way there," Helen said with a grin.

"It's noisy all right," Neil agreed. "It's a good thing we're on the edge of the village — otherwise the neighbors would probably complain."

Inside the rescue center, Neil introduced Helen to the dogs in the first three pens, starting with Sailor, who was bouncing up and down in his pen as if he were on springs.

"He's pretty lively," Helen remarked. "I bet he never gets tired."

"That's probably why he got lost in the first place," Neil pointed out. "Running too fast for his owners to keep up when they took him for a walk."

"He might have been chasing after a rabbit," Helen suggested. "My aunt in Oxford has a Jack Russell and he chases anything he sees. She has to keep him

on one of those retractable leashes so she can reel
him in when she needs to."

"That's a good idea," said Neil. "I'll tell Sailor's owners if we manage to find them."

They patted Nina and Titus, then moved on to
Sapphire and Trick.

"Hey — that's funny," said Neil, staring in confusion at the two dogs.

"What's funny?" Helen asked. The poodle and the
puppy were sitting beside the wire, looking up at the
visitors expectantly.

"They've swapped pens," Neil said, folding his arms
and looking from one dog to the other.

"You're right!" Helen agreed. "We definitely put
Trick in pen number five last night, and now he's in
pen four. What do you think happened?"

"I dunno." Neil shrugged. "Maybe Bev made a mistake when she cleaned out their pens."

"A mistake about what?" said Bev, coming in just
in time to overhear Neil's remark.

Neil pointed at Sapphire and Trick. "These two
have swapped pens," he explained.

"Well, I didn't mix them up," Bev said with a frown.
She looked over to the food preparation area. "Look,
you can see from the notes I made on the black-
board — Sapphire was definitely in pen four. What's
been going on in here?"

As if trying to answer her, the puppy suddenly
picked up Sapphire's dark blue blanket in his mouth.

He dragged it over to the gate, lurching to one side as it became caught up under his paws.

"He wants to give it to us," said Helen, kneeling down and holding out her hand to encourage Trick to come closer.

Neil opened the gate. "Give," he said, gently taking hold of the blanket. Trick opened his mouth and allowed Neil to take it.

"Good boy," said Neil, rubbing the puppy's chest. "You *are* a smart little dog. Now all we need is for you to speak and tell us how you got in here."

"That would be nice." Bev grinned. "And in the meantime, while he's finding his words, we'd better swap them around again. The bed in Sapphire's pen is much too big for that little pup!"

"OK," said Neil. "But before we put Trick back in, we should take a picture of him for the web site."

"In that case, I'll leave you to it," said Bev, glancing at her watch. "I'm going home now." She smiled at Neil. "I know I can trust you to make sure the gates are shut properly."

After Bev had left, Neil took his digital camera out of his jacket pocket while Helen held Trick. "See if you can get him to face me," Neil suggested, sitting on the floor so that the camera was level with the puppy.

Helen pushed Trick down until he sat. Then she backed away from the little dog.

Neil looked through the viewfinder. "Perfect," he

said, clicking the shutter. But in that instant, Trick spotted the interesting-looking box in Neil's hands and trotted over to investigate it.

Neil groaned. "That'll be one big blur," he said, as Trick stood up with his front paws against Neil's chest and sniffed at the camera. Neil let the puppy satisfy his curiosity, then asked Helen to try again. "This time, you'd better hold on to him."

The second attempt was more successful, although as soon as the shutter had clicked, Trick wriggled out of Helen's hands and bounded over again to see what had made the noise.

"You really are inquisitive," Neil remarked, trying to replace the lens cap, which Trick was sniffing with interest. Neil looked across at Sapphire. She was sitting in her pen watching all the activity with her head to one side.

"I think I'll take a photo of you, too," said Neil. "Smile, Sapphire!"

Sapphire pricked up her ears and stayed perfectly still while Neil took the picture. As soon as he lowered the camera, she stood up, her tail wagging.

"She's not camera-shy!" Helen laughed.

"Far from it," said Neil. "She's obviously had her photo taken before."

When Trick and Sapphire were back in their original pens, Neil and Helen went into the house to put the puppy's photograph on the web site.

They found Bob in the kitchen sorting through a box of new leashes and collars that had just arrived.

Neil was still feeling puzzled about how the two dogs had managed to get into each other's pens. He asked his dad if he knew anything about it.

"Nope," Bob replied. "The last time I saw them, Sapphire was definitely in pen four. Next to Titus, right? Maybe Emily did it as a joke," he suggested.

"It couldn't have been Em," Neil said. "She isn't back from soccer practice yet."

"Then I guess it's a mystery!" said Bob. He shrugged and looked down at the box again.

"And it *is* nearly Halloween," Helen put in with a grin. "Weird things are supposed to happen around this time."

Neil laughed. "I guess so. And that reminds me — would you like to come trick-or-treating with us on Friday night?"

"Yes, please." Helen beamed as she followed Neil into the office. "I'll check with Mom and Dad that it's OK. Oh, and I can wear the Halloween costume I made when we lived in America."

Neil plugged the digital camera into the back of the computer and installed the photograph on the web site under the heading "Dog of the Week."

"It's a great picture of him," Helen exclaimed when Trick's image appeared on the screen. The puppy sat with his head to one side, his warm brown eyes looking curiously ahead as he tried to figure out what the little silver box was in front of Neil's face.

"And of you," Neil joked, pointing to Helen's hands, which were barely visible around Trick's body. He was just beginning to type a description of Trick when the phone rang. "You can keep going," he told Helen as he picked up the receiver. "King Street Kennels," he said. "Neil Parker speaking."

"Hello, Neil. This is Mrs. Herson," announced the voice at the other end. "How is Sapphire?"

"She's great," said Neil. "The most well-behaved dog we've ever had here!"

"Yes, I can believe that," Mrs. Herson agreed. In the background, Neil could hear the sound of young children squabbling. "I wish my grandchildren were that good! Actually, the children are one of the reasons I'm phoning. I'm going to have to look after them for at least ten more days because my daughter is still very ill. That means Sapphire will need to stay with you for longer. Is that all right?"

"You bet!" said Neil enthusiastically. The longer the poodle was with them the better, as far as he was concerned. Sapphire wasn't just well behaved, she was a real character.

After he hung up, he watched as Helen finished Trick's write-up. "Don't forget to say how smart he is," Neil prompted.

"I already have," Helen told him, scrolling up to the top of the page. "It's the first thing I wrote."

Neil leaned over Helen's shoulder and read her report. It described Trick perfectly. "I like what you say here about him needing a home where he'll be well trained and have lots of opportunities to practice his retrieving," Neil said. "You know a lot about dogs, don't you?"

"A bit," Helen confessed. "Most of my friends have had dogs. Some acted really out of control because they'd had no training at all. Also, I used to help our neighbor in Eindhoven with her puppy. He was a black Labrador and we taught him all sorts of things. He used to fetch the newspaper from their front step and bring it over to us."

Neil pictured the puppy getting the paper next door and imagined how much Helen must have enjoyed being involved with his training. *Too bad she can't have Trick,* he thought. *Still, a dog is for life — not just a year. It wouldn't be fair to either of them if she had to find a new home for Trick when her dad was transferred to another country.*

CHAPTER FOUR

"**N**eil, would you let Trick into the outside run for a while?" Carole called from the office when Neil came home from school on Tuesday afternoon. "He hasn't had much exercise today. Dad only managed to exercise the bigger dogs before he went out, and Bev had to leave early for the dentist."

Although it was only drizzling now, it had been raining heavily all morning, which meant the dogs in the kennel would have been indoors for most of the day. As he went over to the rescue center with Jake, Neil imagined how frustrating it must be for a puppy like Trick to be cooped up for hours at a time. *I just hope he's not too bored,* he thought.

Jake bounded ahead of him into the round building and Neil followed, pausing at Sapphire's pen. The poodle was curled up in her basket and seemed to be fast asleep. *The best way to deal with bad weather,* thought Neil.

At that moment, Sapphire opened her eyes. Instantly alert, she lifted her head up and looked around. She seemed to relax when she saw who it was and put her head on her paws again, wagging her short, fluffy tail.

"Hello, girl." Neil smiled. "It looks like you're wide awake even when you're asleep!"

Sapphire gave a short bark. Neil was sure she was agreeing with him. "I always knew poodles were smart," he said to her. "I bet I could almost have a conversation with you!" He moved toward Trick's pen. "And how are you today, Trick?" he called.

Neil put his hand on the lever next to Trick's pen that would open the back gate and allow the puppy into the outside run. "OK, boy, I'll open the gate and you can go out." He looked at the basket where he expected to see the puppy curled up.

But Trick wasn't there.

Neil stared into the pen. It was completely empty.

"Now what?" Neil breathed in disbelief. He glanced back at Sapphire's pen, wondering if Trick had ended up there again.

"Trick!" Neil called loudly. "TRICK!"

There was no sign of the pup.

Neil looked around wildly. Jake sensed his anxiety. He whined softly and padded back and forth, sniffing the floor intently.

"Find him, Jake," said Neil, swallowing hard. Unwelcome thoughts flashed through his mind as he imagined what might have happened to the puppy. Could someone have sneaked in and stolen him? Or perhaps he had managed to escape and was now loose on the main road. Or maybe . . .

Neil shook his head. Only one thing was certain. Trick wasn't in his pen. Neil had to find him and there was no time to lose.

"Come on, Jake," he said. As he spun around to go, he glanced once more into the puppy's pen. Beside him, Jake let out an excited bark. Trick was in his pen after all.

"Trick!" Neil gasped in amazement.

Padding over to the gate, the puppy stood up against it and wagged his little tail to show how pleased he was to see Neil and Jake.

Neil shook his head and took a deep breath as relief flooded through him. He reached through the wire and ruffled Trick's silky golden coat. "Thank goodness you're safe."

And then it dawned on him that Trick's coat was wet. Feeling a draft, Neil stood up and looked over at the back of the pen. The gate to the run was open just enough to let a small puppy squeeze through. "You've been outside, haven't you?" Neil exclaimed.

Trick wriggled and squirmed gleefully against the wire as if to say, "Yes. And I had a really good time!"

Neil pushed up the lever and the gate slid shut. "That's all the exercise you're getting today," he said, going over to a cupboard for a towel. "You nearly gave me a heart attack!"

He came back and gingerly entered the pen. "And don't try to slip out between my legs," he warned, quickly closing the gate behind him.

As he dried Trick's coat, Neil wondered who would have left the back gate open. He knew it wouldn't have been Bev — she would never open the gates when it was raining. Perhaps the lever that opened and closed the gate was broken. He would ask his dad to check it.

When he returned to the house, Neil found the rest of the Parker family having hot chocolate at the big kitchen table. A spare place was laid next to Sarah for her imaginary friend. Nobody else was allowed to sit there.

Carole took out a cup for Neil. "I thought you were never coming back in again," she said. "Did Trick need a lot of exercise?"

"No. He exercised himself," Neil said. He filled them in on Trick's mysterious outing.

"Sounds like someone's playing tricks on you," Bob suggested. "Just like someone did to me earlier."

Neil put down his cup of hot cocoa and frowned. "What do you mean, Dad?"

"Well, I went into Compton to go to the supermarket this morning," Bob explained. "When I came home, I was just getting out of the car when Mom called me to the phone." He tugged at his beard. "I ran in, leaving the groceries in the car. When I went back out ten minutes later, the shopping bags were gone." He paused and bit into a piece of fruitcake.

"What happened to them?" Neil prompted impatiently.

Bob swallowed the cake. "You won't believe this," he said, "but they were in the kitchen."

"Mom must have brought them in," Emily said at once.

Carole shook her head. "Not guilty." She grinned. "I was in the office the entire time Dad was on the phone."

"Someone else must have been here, then," Neil said. "I mean, shopping bags can't just move on their own."

"That's what I thought," said Bob, pouring another cup of hot cocoa. "But there wasn't anyone else at home then. Except Bev. And she was busy grooming Ben. So it definitely wasn't her."

Ben was a very hairy Old English sheepdog belonging to Emily's best friend, Julie Baker, who was visiting her grandparents this week with the rest of her family. Neil knew Ben needed lots of grooming, so he wasn't surprised that Bev had been busy. He shook his head in disbelief. "Someone's definitely playing tricks on us. I wonder who it is?"

Bob and Carole shrugged. "Some practical joker?" Carole suggested.

"Or," said Emily, her voice quivering with excitement, "a poltergeist!"

"What's a *pottergeist*?" asked Sarah, her mouth full of cake.

"A *pol*tergeist is a naughty, noisy ghost that moves things around and opens and shuts doors," Carole explained. "And you can't see them."

"Just like your secret friend." Emily chuckled.

"My friend's *not* naughty and she's *not* a ghost!" Sarah said with a pout.

"In that case, we definitely can't blame her." Bob grinned. "Perhaps Emily is right and there is a poltergeist around."

Neil wrinkled his nose and shook his head. "I doubt it," he said. "After all, Jake's behaving normally." The Border collie was snoozing in his basket in the corner. Neil went on. "If there really was a ghost around, Jake and the other dogs would be the first to know."

"Mmm," Bob murmured. "You've got a point there. Animals can often see and hear things humans can't. And I haven't noticed any of the dogs acting strangely lately."

"Which means you're probably right, Mom. There must be a practical joker around," said Neil.

*   *   *

The next afternoon, Neil took Jake, Sapphire, and Trick into the field for a run. Let loose in the big area, the three dogs raced and tumbled around until they were panting heavily.

Neil ran with them until he was out of breath, too. Then he called them back to him and gave them each a dog treat. "Let's take a rest," he puffed.

Sapphire shot him a quick look and immediately lay down.

"Wow!" said Neil. "You must have learned the word *rest*." He turned to Jake and Trick. "What about you two? Can you *rest*?"

Two pairs of dark brown eyes studied Neil's face for a second and then the two dogs spun around and hurtled across the field, Trick leaping up at Jake's side.

Sapphire watched them go and glanced up at Neil, her body trembling slightly as she waited eagerly for him to send her off, too. "Go on!" Neil laughed. "Catch them."

Sapphire leaped to her feet and tore after the others.

When the three dogs had had enough exercise, Neil returned Sapphire and Trick to their pens and went into Red's Barn. He had promised to help his dad by making sure everything was ready for the obedience class that Bob Parker held every Wednesday evening.

"I think that's everything," Neil said to Jake as he set out six wooden dumbbells on a bale of straw. "Let's go in for something to drink."

He went into the kitchen, where he found Carole looking very puzzled. "What's the matter, Mom?" Neil asked. He slipped off his damp shoes and left them next to Emily's sneakers in front of the heater.

"I can't find my handbag," Carole told him as she hunted around the kitchen. "I left it here on the table not more than fifteen minutes ago."

"Are you sure?" Neil asked, looking around the room.

"Positive," Carole replied.

Emily came downstairs a few minutes later. "What are you looking for?" she asked as Neil crawled out from under the table.

"Mom's handbag," he told her, rubbing his head where he'd bumped it against a chair leg.

"But it's in your bedroom, Mom," said Emily. "I just saw it there."

"In my bedroom?" Carole frowned. "It can't be. I know I left it here."

Shrugging, she went upstairs. Neil followed her, raising his eyebrows at Emily. Sure enough, the black bag was lying on the bed.

Carole shook her head in bewilderment. "How in the world did it get here?" she said. "I know I left it on the kitchen table after I picked up Sarah from her swimming lesson." She thought for a moment. "I haven't even been up here since I got back. I loaded the washing machine, then went straight into the office."

"Maybe Sarah brought it up," Emily suggested.

Carole smiled. "Maybe she did. I'll ask her." She picked up the bag and went out into the hallway. "Sarah!" she called.

The little girl appeared at the bottom of the stairs. "Yes, Mom?"

"Did you put my bag on my bed?" Carole asked.

Sarah shook her head. "No. It was Misty," she said confidently.

"Misty?" Carole echoed.

"Yes," said Sarah. "I saw her putting it there. She's very smart, you know."

"Seems like it," said Carole with a grin, going back downstairs and taking her car keys out of her bag. "Well, at least we've solved the mystery. Now, Sarah,

I hope you — and, of course . . ." she paused and winked at Neil and Emily, "your friend *Misty* — are ready. We must go now or we'll be late for the rehearsal."

Sarah's ballet class was practicing for a special Halloween concert they were to perform on Saturday. Emily had volunteered to help backstage, so she was going along, too. "I'll just get my shoes," said Emily. "They should be dry by now." She hurried into the kitchen.

Moments later, Neil heard a puzzled, "Hey!"

"What's the matter, Em?" he asked, going into the kitchen.

"My sneakers," she said, looking around in bewilderment. "Have you seen them?"

Neil looked over at the heater. There were no shoes in sight — not even his, which he'd left there only ten minutes before. "This is getting ridiculous," he said as Sarah came in with her ballet bag. "Are you the shoe thief, too?" he demanded.

"I didn't steal your shoes," Sarah protested, folding her arms in anger. "They're on the porch."

"But we put them in front of the heater to dry out, Squirt," Emily told her. "Why did you move them?"

"I didn't. Misty took them to the porch. I think she thought they looked untidy in here."

"Give me a break, Squirt!" Neil laughed. "You can't fool us. It's too early for Halloween ghosts. Wait until Friday."

Sarah put her hands on her hips and glared at Neil. "But Misty *did* move your shoes. I saw her. She does lots of things in the house."

"Yeah, I'm sure," Neil joked. But he had to admit to himself that something odd was definitely going on at King Street Kennels. He didn't think Sarah could be moving the dogs around as well.

Neil shrugged, putting the strange events in the back of his mind. After all, there were more important things to think about — like Trick. Shutting the front door behind his mom, Emily, and Sarah, he went into the office with Jake to check the e-mails.

There were several from people who wanted to know more about the little retriever cross. Neil was glad that there was so much interest in the puppy, but he guessed that Helen would probably be pretty sad when Trick finally went to a new home.

Neil had just finished printing out the e-mails when he heard a thud, followed by a low humming noise. It seemed to be coming from the utility room.

"What's that, Jake?" he said to the dog, who was lying at his feet. Jake opened his eyes and blinked sleepily at Neil, then went back to sleep. *He* hadn't noticed anything out of the ordinary.

But the droning sound continued. "It can't be Dad," Neil said. "He's in the barn with his class. I guess I'd better go and check. Come on, Jake."

With the Border collie padding quietly behind him, Neil went to investigate. The kitchen was dark, but there was a light on in the utility room. As Neil crossed the kitchen to see who was there, the light was suddenly switched off.

"Who's there?" Neil called out.

There was no reply. And then, above the humming noise, Neil heard a distinct click — like the sound of the back door closing. He swallowed and looked down at Jake. The Border collie wagged his tail calmly. He was completely unperturbed.

"OK," said Neil, taking a deep breath. If Jake wasn't worried, neither was he. "Let's go in."

He stepped into the utility room, switched on the light, and gasped. The room was empty, but someone had definitely just been there. The washing machine door was wide open. And the clothes that Carole had put into the wash that afternoon were now churning around in the dryer!

CHAPTER FIVE

Neil was gripped by icy fear. This was definitely more than just a practical joke. Who would come all the way to King Street Kennels on a cold, dark evening just to play a prank? *And this time,* thought Neil, *we can't blame "Misty" because Squirt's not here.*

Slowly he backed out of the utility room, trying to convince himself that his mom must have transferred the clothes and switched on the dryer on her way out. But Neil knew that that wasn't what had happened. He'd seen his mom go out the front door — she hadn't gone anywhere near the utility room.

So who was responsible? *Dad? Impossible,* thought Neil. *He'd never come in halfway through an obedience class just to put clothes in the dryer.*

Then he remembered Emily's suggestion that there

might be a poltergeist at King Street Kennels. Could she be right? That would certainly explain the way things kept disappearing and then turning up somewhere completely different. But if there was a real ghost around, wouldn't Jake have barked?

Neil went back to the office and tried to concentrate as he read through the e-mails. But his mind kept drifting back to the strange goings-on. There had to be a simple explanation for them. But what could it be?

Later that evening, Neil was in the living room doing his homework when he heard his mom and his sisters return.

Carole put her head in the door. "Hot chocolate, Neil?" she offered.

"Yes, please, Mom," he said, putting away his work and going into the kitchen, where Emily was placing five mugs on the table.

"The fifth cup is for?" Neil asked, helping himself to one of the mugs.

"My friend," Sarah replied seriously. She pulled out two chairs, then climbed onto one and began a conversation with the invisible person sitting next to her. She took a sip from her mug, then leaned over to drink from the other one.

"It looks like your friend can't manage her drink on her own," said Carole. "Why don't we let Dad help her?" She looked up at the clock. "His class will be over soon."

Bob came in a few minutes later. He looked tired and reached gratefully for the extra cup of hot cocoa. "I need this after that class," he groaned. "They're a demanding group — especially that big Doberman who joined two weeks ago. He's way too strong for his owner. I don't know why a small woman wants such an enormous dog." He helped himself to a cookie, then asked, "Any e-mails about Trick, Neil?"

"A lot," said Neil. "I've printed them out for you." He paused, wondering if he should tell the others about the mysterious incident in the utility room. *I might as well,* he decided, still convinced there was a perfectly logical explanation for it.

He described what he had heard and turned to Bob. "You didn't come in and turn on the dryer, did you, Dad?"

Bob looked surprised. "Me? No chance of that. I couldn't leave the barn for a second this evening — not with that Doberman behaving so badly."

"So if you didn't turn on the dryer," Neil continued, "who did?"

Bob shrugged and winked at Sarah. "Maybe it was Misty again."

"I bet it was," said Sarah. "She likes to help out."

"Well, it's nice to have a helpful ghost," Carole said with a smile, "but I'm not sure I want her interfering with the housework again!"

"I hope she doesn't," said Neil. "All this sneaky 'help' is beginning to give me the creeps!"

                    *   *   *

Neil heaved the pumpkin onto the kitchen table in front of Sarah. "There, Squirt," he said. "See what you can do with that."

"Yes," said Emily. "Maybe your friend can help you!"

It was late Thursday evening and the Parkers were busy with their final preparations for Halloween.

Sarah picked up a carving knife and was about to plunge it into the pumpkin when Bob leaned forward and stopped her. "Here, let me help you with that," he said. "You don't want to hurt yourself."

"I won't," Sarah protested.

"Well, then let's make sure your friend doesn't get hurt," said Bob firmly, taking the knife and slicing the top off the pumpkin.

There was a knock on the back door. It was Helen arriving for her daily visit with Trick.

"Let me guess," said Carole as Helen came in. "You're not here to carve a pumpkin for tomorrow night, are you?"

Helen smiled and shook her head. Neil grinned at her and got up to take her out to the kennel block.

"I don't blame you," Carole went on. "That puppy's a real cutie pie."

"Why don't we try some training with him tonight?" Neil suggested, turning to Emily and Helen. "We'll take him and Jake into Red's Barn."

"That'd be great!" Helen said.

At the sound of his name, Jake leaped out of his

basket in the corner and tore over to Neil, his tail wagging frantically.

Neil ruffled Jake's shaggy fur. "OK, boy. We're going in a minute."

"Why don't we take Sapphire, too?" Emily suggested. "You said she really enjoyed playing with Jake and Trick yesterday."

"Good idea," said Neil, nodding.

Inside Red's Barn, the three dogs soon picked up the scents left behind by the members of the previous night's class and began nosing around inquisitively.

"What should we teach them first?" asked Helen.

Neil noticed that Trick had picked up one of the wooden dumbbells. "Let's concentrate on retrieving," he said. "Trick has a really strong instinct for it."

"I'd love to see that!" Helen beamed.

They called the dogs back to them and held on to them. But Trick had too much energy to stay still for long. He squirmed around until he managed to free himself from Helen's hands, then he flopped down at her feet and rolled around in the sand.

"I think he's too busy taking a sand bath to be interested in retrieving now," Helen observed.

"Well, I'll show you what I've been trying to teach Jake," said Neil. He went over to a large wooden chest and took out a few items — another wooden dumbbell, an old shoe, a Frisbee, and a stainless steel bowl. He arranged them in a row on the ground in front of

Jake. "I want him to learn to fetch the dish for me," Neil explained to Emily and Helen.

"You mean he has to learn the names of different objects?" Helen asked. She sounded impressed.

"Yep," said Neil. "He already knows *fetch,* but now I want him to choose a particular item. OK, Jake," he said, getting his dog's attention again. "Listen to me." He pointed to the bowl and said, "Dish."

The Border collie sniffed it hopefully and looked up at Neil.

Neil took him back a few feet. "Now, Jake," he said, letting go of his collar. "Fetch the *dish.*"

Eagerly, Jake trotted across the barn and without hesitating picked up the first item he came to: the Frisbee. With his tail wagging proudly, he bounded over to Neil and dropped the plastic toy at his feet.

"Thanks, but no thanks," Neil said patiently. "That's a *Frisbee.*" He put it back with the other items, then repeated the command. "Dish," he stressed. "Fetch the *dish.*"

Jake set off once more and quickly returned — this time with the dumbbell.

Emily laughed. "I don't blame him. I'd hate to pick up a cold metal bowl in my mouth." She pretended to shudder, momentarily letting go of Sapphire's collar just as Neil tossed the dumbbell back and urged Jake to have another go.

"Fetch the *dish,*" he said firmly.

But this time it wasn't Jake who responded. It was

Sapphire. With her elegant head held high, she trotted over to the objects and inspected each one before confidently picking up the stainless steel bowl. Then she raced back to Neil and sat squarely in front of him, offering him the bowl in her mouth.

"Wow!" said Helen. "That's amazing."

Neil was equally impressed. "Good girl," he said, taking the dish from Sapphire and rewarding her with a dog treat. "Did you see that, Jake?" he said, pretending to sound stern.

Jake thumped his tail up and down and let out a series of short barks.

"Let's see if she'll do it again," said Emily.

"OK," Neil agreed. "Fetch the dish," he repeated. Sapphire went like an arrow to the steel bowl and brought it back again.

"She definitely knows what she's doing," said Neil admiringly. He patted the poodle's woolly head. "Do you want to fetch something else for me?" he asked, taking the bowl from her.

Sapphire wagged her tail enthusiastically and watched eagerly as Neil replaced the bowl.

"Let's try the shoe this time," Helen suggested.

But this time someone else wanted a turn. Yapping excitedly, Trick leaped up and hurtled over to the row of objects. With an agile dive, he pounced onto them and seized the first thing he found. It was the shoe. Gripping it in his teeth, he backed up a few paces, then turned and ran toward Helen.

Helen gasped. "That's amazing!" she cried. "He must have heard me say *shoe!*"

But she'd hardly stopped talking before Trick dropped the shoe at her feet and, spinning around, bounced back to the other objects. This time he picked up a box, then went scampering over to a corner where he lay down and began to shred the cardboard with his sharp little teeth.

"I should have guessed he was just playing!" Helen laughed.

"Yes," said Emily, going over to remove the box before Trick managed to swallow any of it. "I don't think he'll make Dad's advanced class yet!"

"No, but he has a lot of potential," said Neil. "He's a sharp dog!"

CHAPTER SIX

Dressed in his skeleton sweatshirt and black jeans, Neil put the hollowed-out pumpkin on the window-sill and lit the candle inside it. Then he switched off the kitchen light and went out into the front yard, where Emily, Sarah, and Helen were waiting for him. It was Friday night and the four of them were about to go into Compton on their Halloween outing.

"Ooh!" Sarah squealed. "It's really spooky!"

The flickering candlelight inside the pumpkin shell made the scary face that Bob and Sarah had carved look very dramatic.

"It looks like a monster waiting to gobble us up," said Sarah, her voice quivering with excitement. She hopped from one foot to the other and pulled at Neil's sleeve. "Let's go," she said impatiently.

"OK, OK!" Neil grinned, bending down to clip the leash onto Jake's collar.

"I'm so glad he's coming, too," said Helen, giving Jake a quick pat.

"Yes. He can protect us from all the ghosts," Emily joked, adjusting her pointed hat. It kept slipping down one side of her head.

"Maybe a real ghost will do a better job of that," Neil said with a chuckle. He turned to Sarah. "Is Misty coming with us, Squirt?" he asked.

Sarah gave him an indignant look. "Don't be ridiculous," she said in her most grown-up voice. "Misty has to stay at home. Don't you know anything?"

"Sorry," said Neil hastily. "But I thought you said you were making her a costume last Sunday."

Sarah folded her arms and frowned at Neil. "That's silly," she said.

Neil shrugged and picked up his basket. Bob came out of the house to join them and they headed down the driveway with Jake pulling excitedly at the end of his leash.

"Who's going to be our first victim?" Emily asked.

"How about Smiler?" suggested Neil. Smiler was the nickname given to Mr. Hamley, the principal at Meadowbank School. He owned a friendly but disobedient Dalmatian called Dotty.

"Perfect!" Emily exclaimed. "Now's our chance to get back at him for being so strict all the time."

"Do you think that's a good idea?" Helen asked hesitantly.

"He's not that bad," Neil reassured her. "Anyone who loves a dog as much as Smiler loves Dotty *has* to be a nice person."

They arrived at Mr. Hamley's house and marched up to the front door, leaving Bob waiting behind the bushes. Neil rang the bell. There was a sharp bark from inside and then a woman's voice called out, "Who is it?"

"Trick or treat?" Neil answered loudly.

The door opened. A blur of white and black shot out and leaped playfully at Jake.

"Inside, Dotty!" said Mrs. Hamley, hurrying after her.

But the Dalmatian ignored her. Jake was much more interesting.

"I've got her!" Emily gasped.

Mrs. Hamley reached over and held on to the Dalmatian. "She just adores visitors — especially canine ones," she said, laughing.

"Who's there, Rachel?" came Mr. Hamley's voice.

"A bunch of witches and other scary creatures!" Mrs. Hamley chuckled.

The principal appeared on the doorstep behind his wife. "So, you think you can trick us into giving you a treat?" he said sternly to the group standing in front of him.

Neil noticed Helen's face drop. He nudged her lightly with his elbow. Although the teacher sounded serious, Neil could see a twinkle in his eyes and the beginning of a smile at the corners of his mouth.

Unlike Helen, Sarah wasn't at all put off by his stern words. "Trick or treat?" she reminded him impatiently.

Mr. Hamley's face lit up as a broad grin spread across it. "Treat!" he declared. He picked up four brown paper bags from a table in the hall and handed them over. "I'll remember this on Monday when you're at school — under *my* control," he added, his eyes twinkling.

Neil looked in his bag and then up at Mr. Hamley and his wife. Laughing, he replied, "Thanks for the peanuts, sir."

"Ugh," Sarah grumbled at his side. "I hate peanuts."

"Sshh," said Emily. "You can swap them with me later."

The next stop was Dr. Harvey's house. The large, untidy man appeared at his front door flanked by his two dogs — Sandy, his well-behaved mongrel, and Finn, his pedigree Kerry blue terrier, who squirmed with delight when he saw Jake.

"Will these do?" Dr. Harvey asked doubtfully, holding out a handful of Gummi Bears. Neil was sure they came from the jar on the doctor's desk in his office. "I was so busy today I didn't have time to go shopping for anything."

"They're just fine," said Neil. "Better than cough drops or vitamin pills!" he joked.

Next, they moved on to Kate and Glen Paget's cottage. "Let's play a trick on them," Neil suggested.

"OK," said Bob. "But nothing too outrageous."

"What sort of trick?" Helen asked.

"We'll all creep away and leave Jake at the door," said Neil. "That should confuse them."

Bob and the three girls hid behind the bushes while Neil took Jake up the path and rang the doorbell. "Stay, Jake," he whispered to his dog, before dashing off to join the others. Jake sat still, looking after Neil with a confused expression on his face.

They heard the door open, then Kate's surprised voice saying, "Jake! What are you doing here?" This was followed by the sound of pattering footsteps.

Neil peeped around the bushes and saw Jake running toward him — with Kate right behind! "You silly dog!" Neil laughed as the Border collie ran up to him, his mouth wide open in a cheerful doggy grin. "You weren't supposed to give away that we were here."

Kate folded her arms across her swollen tummy. "I think I would have figured out that you were somewhere nearby," she said with a chuckle. "After all, Jake's never too far from you, Neil."

Several stops later, they came to the police station. "Let's go in," Neil said. "We can check whether anyone's been asking for Trick." Even though he strongly suspected the puppy had been abandoned, there was still a chance that Trick may have wandered off from his owners.

"People don't ask for tricks on Halloween," Sarah objected. "Treats are much nicer!"

"I'm talking about Trick, the puppy Helen found," Neil explained as he opened the door.

Inside, it was warm and cozy. Neil glanced at the bulletin board. The photograph of Trick that he'd brought by earlier in the week was still there.

"Hello there," said Sergeant Moorhead, who was sitting behind the counter. "What can I . . . Oh, I see! It's trick or treat, isn't it?"

They nodded and Sarah heaved her basket onto the counter.

"Well, I don't have any candy, but let me treat you to some hot chocolate instead. You all look frozen," said the policeman.

Soon they were sitting on the bench beside the counter, drinking from huge blue mugs filled with steaming hot chocolate. Jake lay quietly at Neil's feet, his eyes fixed firmly on the sergeant's police dog, Sherlock, who sat proudly next to his master's chair.

Helen admired the handsome German shepherd. "Is he friendly?" she asked.

"Oh yes," said the sergeant. "But he's also an excellent police dog."

"I wish he could track down Trick's owner," Helen said quietly.

"Why? To arrest him?" asked Neil.

"Maybe," Helen admitted. "Or perhaps he could sniff out a loving home for Trick."

"Still no luck?" asked Sergeant Moorhead.

"Nothing," said Neil. "He's been with us for five whole days now. I was hoping you might have some news for us."

Sergeant Moorhead shook his head. "Not a word about any missing dogs." He looked across at the photograph. "But I'm sure a handsome little guy like him will soon find a new home."

*   *   *

As they turned back toward home, a thick mist began to gather. Helen suggested they tell each other ghost stories. Neil's tale was particularly scary. It was about a phantom dog — a huge bloodhound that roamed the streets of the town, unable to rest until a wicked, dog-hating witch was driven out.

Soon they came to the road leading to Helen's house. "Thanks for letting me come," she said, waving goodbye. "See you tomorrow."

"Yes. And don't forget we're taking Trick and Jake for a walk in the park," Neil called after her.

By the time they arrived at King Street Kennels, the mist had thickened. It swirled around the security lights like steam rising from a cauldron. From the kitchen window, the pumpkin grinned eerily.

As soon as Carole heard them crunching up the driveway, she opened the kitchen door. A pool of warm light spilled out into the dark yard. "Have fun?" she asked.

"Ooh, yes," said Sarah, holding out her basket. "Look at all my candy!"

"I hope you're not going to eat all of that yourself," said Carole, ushering Sarah into the kitchen.

"No. I'm going to share it." Sarah announced, trying unsuccessfully to stifle a big yawn.

"I'm sure Misty will appreciate that," said Carole with a smile.

Through another huge yawn, Sarah said seriously, "Misty isn't allowed to eat candy."

"Very convenient." Neil grinned, then turned to Emily. "Let's check the kennel before we go in," he suggested. "Just in case that bloodhound's been here!"

They took Jake inside and dumped their baskets on the kitchen table before heading back out into the courtyard again.

"This fog's so thick, I can hardly see a thing," Emily complained as they approached the kennel block.

"Me, neither," said Neil. And then he froze. Something was moving rapidly through the mist. "Look, Em!" he breathed, feeling his heart miss a beat.

Ahead of them, a pale, ghostly shape flitted silently toward the rescue center before disappearing into the shadows.

CHAPTER SEVEN

Neil's first thought was of the dogs. Whatever he'd seen had been heading straight for them. Neil charged toward the kennel door. "Quick, Em!" he cried.

"But what if it's —" Emily began anxiously.

Neil cut in. "I don't care what it is," he said. "We've got to make sure the dogs are safe."

They burst into the rescue block and Neil switched on the lights. The sudden brightness woke up the dogs. They lifted their heads and looked at Neil and Emily, blinking sleepily. All the dogs looked fine. Nothing seemed to have upset them.

"Everything's OK, I think." Neil sighed with relief. "But let's check each pen anyway." He stopped in front of the first pen and tested the latch on the gate.

Sailor sprang out of his basket and scampered over, his muscular little body trembling with excitement.

"Sorry, Sailor," said Neil, crouching down to touch the Jack Russell through the wire. "We're only here to make sure you're OK."

"I'll give them some treats so they won't be disappointed," Emily said, going into the food preparation area.

Neil stood up and glanced around. Everything looked perfectly normal. *It must have just been a shadow of a tree — or even a big swirl of mist*, he thought. After all those spooky stories, maybe their imaginations were on overdrive!

He looked into Titus's pen. The bullmastiff stared back at Neil from his basket, his handsome black face wrinkled in a frown. "It's OK," Neil murmured. "You can go back to sleep now, Titus. And you, Sapphire . . ." he went on, looking into the next pen.

His heart lurched. Sapphire wasn't there. But sitting happily in her basket was Trick!

Neil's eyes grew wide. "Em!" he gasped. Then he glanced over into Trick's pen. And there, curled up peacefully in the undersized puppy bed, was the poodle.

"I don't understand," said Neil, shaking his head in confusion. "How does this keep happening?" A chill ran down his spine as he pictured again the mysterious moving shape in the courtyard. Was it just a coincidence, or were these two events related?

Emily came hurrying back with a bowl full of treats. She stopped next to Neil and her mouth dropped as she stared at the two dogs. Finally, with a trembling voice, she managed to whisper, "This can't be a joke."

Neil had to agree. Everything was beginning to point to something much more bizarre than a few simple tricks.

"Do you think," Emily began hesitantly, "that there *is* a poltergeist here after all?"

Neil didn't know *what* to think anymore. He rubbed his eyes, then took a deep breath, trying to clear his mind. He decided to fetch Jake. "If there *is* someone or something strange around, he'll track it down," he said confidently.

They went back to the house to get the Border collie. Bob was sitting at the kitchen table reading the newspaper and snacking on the Halloween candy. "What's up?" he asked, with his mouth full. "You both look as if you've seen a ghost."

"Funny you should say that, Dad," said Neil. "Because . . ." He paused, wondering how to make his father take him seriously.

"We think we *did* just see one," Emily burst out. "Near the rescue kennel."

Bob grinned at her. "You don't think you've just been telling too many ghost stories?"

"We did see something weird," Neil insisted. "It was sort of shadowy and silent. And then we found Trick and Sapphire in each other's pens again."

Bob frowned at Neil. "Are you sure?" he asked.

Neil nodded solemnly.

Bob fell silent for a moment. Then, shrugging his shoulders, he said, "I can't understand how those two keep getting swapped." He helped himself to a handful of peanuts. "I'm sure there's a simple explanation for it. And as for your spooky sighting," he added, "it could have been a fox, a badger, or even a stray dog that was attracted by the scent of all the other dogs."

"If it was," said Neil, looking over to his own dog, who was lying in his basket in the corner, "then Jake should be able to sniff it out." He clapped his hands together. "Come on, boy. Let's find it!"

Jake jumped up and ran over to him.

"Coming, Em?" asked Neil, opening the door.

Emily hesitated for a moment. Then she took off her witch's hat, put it on the table, and followed her brother back out into the foggy night.

First, they took Jake into the kennel blocks. Jake looked a little puzzled at being taken to see the boarders at that time of night, but he went over and greeted the dogs enthusiastically.

"He doesn't look too bothered by anything in here," said Emily.

"I guess not," Neil agreed. He began to wonder if Bob had been right, and if a stray dog had been snooping around. It might be in the fields behind the kennel. In that case, the poor animal had to be found. It would be hungry and possibly even frightened. "Let's try the field," he suggested.

They trudged around the dark, muddy field with Jake weaving back and forth in front of them. Finally, Neil had to accept defeat. "I guess we'll never know," he admitted. "It probably *was* just my imagination."

"But we both saw it," Emily insisted as they went through the gate and headed back to the house. "And then it disappeared again — just like a ghost."

*   *   *

"Which dogs would you like to feed?" Neil asked Emily the next morning. They were crossing the courtyard to the kennel block. As usual, Jake bounded around them, investigating all the smells in the yard.

"It doesn't matter to me," said Emily. "Maybe the boarders."

Being Saturday, it was Bev's morning off, so Neil and Emily were seeing to the residents while Carole and Sarah helped Mike Turner with his regular dog clinic.

Neil left Emily at the boarding kennel and went into the rescue center. Jake trotted in with him and greeted his friends in their pens while Neil prepared their food.

"Here you are," said Neil, entering Sapphire's enclosure and putting the dish of food on the floor for her. She glanced up at him and then dove into her food, her stumpy tail wagging furiously.

Next, Neil took Trick his breakfast. The pup attacked the food, wolfing it down as if he hadn't eaten for a week.

"Take it easy!" said Neil. "You'll make yourself sick."

But Trick had no intention of slowing down. In less than a minute he had gobbled up all his food. He licked the bowl, making sure not a speck remained, then looked up hopefully at Neil.

Neil patted the puppy and picked up his dish. "That's all for now, Trick," he told him with a grin. He collected the rest of the bowls and took them to the work area. He was about to start washing them when he heard a soft click and a small creaking sound.

Instantly, the vision of the previous night flooded back into his mind. He spun around. The gate to Sapphire's pen was swinging open. Neil held his breath. There was no one else around — no one who could have opened the gate!

And then, before Neil could run to close the pen, Sapphire stepped out into the aisle.

Neil was about to make a dash to grab her, but she seemed to know exactly where she was going. Keeping well back, he tiptoed after her.

The poodle came to the door of the yard. To Neil's astonishment, Sapphire stood up on her hind legs and pushed down the handle with one of her front paws before nudging the door open with her nose.

Neil followed Sapphire outside and saw her trotting purposefully across the courtyard toward the back door. He paused to see if she would open that, too.

She did. And without hesitating, she went inside.

What does she want in there? Neil wondered. He stood on the back step and peered through the open door. He could hardly believe his eyes. Sapphire was in the utility room and she was dragging an empty laundry basket across to the dryer. Neil felt baffled. What in the world was she doing?

Sapphire soon provided the answer. As Neil watched

openmouthed, the extraordinary poodle tugged open the door to the dryer with one paw. Then she gently began pulling out the clean laundry with her mouth and dropping it into the basket!

CHAPTER EIGHT

The others have got to see this, thought Neil. *Or else they'll never believe me.*

Silently he backed away. *Why would she want to unload the laundry?* he asked himself as he slipped away. *It's not exactly natural behavior!*

Deep in thought, he crept through the kitchen, along the hall, and into the sitting room, where his dad was chatting with Terri McCall from the SPCA.

"Hi!" said Neil breathlessly. He beckoned to them. "Quick! Come and —"

"Terri's here to meet Trick," Bob said cheerfully before Neil could go on. "So that she can identify him if anyone comes asking about him."

Neil nodded impatiently. "Come and see this," he repeated. "But don't make a noise."

Bob raised his eyebrows and shrugged. "Sometimes I think I'm the only sane one around here," he whispered to Terri with a grin. "You should hear what's been going on all week." They tiptoed into the kitchen.

In the utility room, Sapphire was still engrossed in her task. When she realized she had an audience, she cast them a casual sideways glance before reaching into the dryer for the last item.

"Isn't that amazing!" Neil murmured as Sapphire reemerged from the machine with a sock in her mouth.

Having emptied the dryer, Sapphire pushed the door closed with her nose. Next, she gripped the handle of the basket in her teeth and pulled it across to Neil.

"Thank you, Sapphire," said Neil. He gently patted her curly neck. "I always knew poodles were smart!"

Sapphire looked at Neil, her dark eyes twinkling happily. Then she sat down and offered him her paw.

"And now you're giving me a high five!" Neil laughed, taking the paw in his hand. "You're amazing!"

Terri was smiling broadly. "I think you've hit the nail on the head there, Neil. This is no ordinary dog."

"What do you mean?" Neil frowned.

Terri listed the poodle's good points. "She's intelligent, helpful, and shows a lot of initiative." Terri took her car keys out of her pocket and dropped them on the floor. At once, Sapphire sprang forward and picked them up, then presented them to Terri. "Good girl," said Terri, taking the keys from her. She looked at Neil and Bob. "I thought she'd do that. You see, I think she's been trained as an assistance dog."

"You mean, her owner taught her to help him around the house?" Neil asked.

"Well, it's probably not as simple as that," said Terri. "What do you know about Sapphire's owner?"

"Nothing really," Bob admitted. "She was brought in by someone else. A friend, I believe. Why do you ask?"

"Because I think Sapphire lives with a disabled person," said Terri. "That's why she knows how to unload the laundry. It's my guess she's been trained by an organization like Canine Partners for Independence to do all sorts of things for someone in a wheelchair."

Neil was fascinated. He had learned about guide dogs for the blind when he met Chloe, a yellow Labrador that belonged to his friend Charlie. But this was the first time he'd heard about dogs being trained to help people in wheelchairs. He looked at Sapphire with renewed respect. "You must be a very important dog," he said.

Behind them, the kitchen door suddenly burst open. "Dad! Neil!" Emily cried out as she rushed in with Sarah behind her. "Mike wanted to check Sapphire, but she's not . . ." She stopped abruptly when she saw the poodle standing next to Neil. "*There* you are." She sighed with relief. "We thought you'd disappeared!"

"Misty!" Sarah exclaimed, running over to Sapphire and wrapping her arms around the poodle's neck. "Have you come to help us again?"

Bob looked utterly bewildered. He glanced back and forth between Sarah and Emily, his face creased in confusion. "Misty? Sapphire lost? What are you two talking about?" he asked.

But for Neil, things were suddenly crystal clear. "Sapphire's our poltergeist!" he said, laughing. "And she's 'Misty,' too!" He turned to his little sister. "You were right the other day, Squirt. Misty — also known as Sapphire — has been doing lots of things in the house, like putting away our shoes and carrying Dad's shopping in from the car. *She's* not your invisible friend after all. And now we know who kept opening the pens in the rescue center! So you see, we aren't being haunted by a Halloween poltergeist at all!"

Sarah nodded knowingly. "Misty's very smart. She even helped me when I was cleaning out Fudge's cage the other day." Fudge was Sarah's pet hamster.

"What did she do?" Emily asked.

"She carried a bag of sawdust to the cage for me," Sarah told her.

Bob looked impressed. "Didn't she puncture it with her teeth?"

"Nope," said Sarah. "She knows how to carry things properly."

"I can believe that," said Neil. Turning to Emily,

he filled her in on what Terri had just told him about Sapphire.

Emily listened in amazement. When Neil had finished, she hugged Sapphire affectionately. "And to think we accused you of being a poltergeist!"

"Will someone *please* tell me what all this is about Misty and poltergeists?" begged Terri just as Mike Turner entered the kitchen. "Otherwise I'll burst from curiosity."

"Curiosity about what?" asked the vet. Then he noticed Sapphire. "Ah! Good! There she is."

Neil quickly explained what had been going on at King Street the last few days.

"No wonder you thought there was a ghost haunt-

ing the place!" Terri said when Neil had finished. "But why do you call her Misty, Sarah?"

"Because her coat is the same color as mist, of course," said Sarah.

"Which is why we thought she was a ghost when we saw her sneaking across the courtyard in the fog last night!" Neil chuckled. He patted Sapphire. "Sorry, girl," he said. "We didn't mean to insult you."

In reply, Sapphire sat back on her haunches, then lifted both paws and gently rested them on Neil's arm. She barked softly, as if to say, "That's OK. I understand."

While Carole was making lunch and Sarah was playing with her invisible friend, Neil and Emily decided to search the Internet to find out more about assistance dogs. Neil logged on to the Canine Partners for Independence web site and discovered that there was a branch not far from them, in Padsham. "A man called Dave Morris is the local organizer," he read out.

"Let's call him," Emily suggested. "He probably knows Sapphire and he might let us visit to find out more about assistance dogs."

Neil quickly dialed the number given on the web site.

"Sapphire?" said a friendly voice after Neil had explained why he was calling. "I know her very well. She's Kevin Dunbar's dog. He's in a wheelchair because of a car accident a few years ago. But thanks to Sapphire, he leads a very busy life."

"She's an incredible dog," Neil agreed.

"More than incredible," Dave told him. "She's one of the best. In fact, she's quite a celebrity. She and Kevin are practically famous these days."

Neil wished he could see them together. "Is Kevin still in the hospital?" he asked.

"Yes," said Dave. "He should have left Sapphire with his appointed support person."

"That'd be Mrs. Herson," said Neil. "But she had a family crisis, and that's why she had to leave Sapphire with us." He told Dave what had happened the previous Sunday night when Mrs. Herson had arrived at King Street Kennels.

There was a slight pause before Dave replied. "That is a bit irregular," he said. "We don't usually like our dogs to be left elsewhere, and we have an emergency service for this type of situation."

Neil thought he sounded anxious, but before he could reassure him about King Street Kennels, Dave went on. "But considering the circumstances, I understand that Mrs. Herson had no choice and that she surely left Sapphire in very good hands."

"I promise you she did," Neil said confidently. "But you can come see for yourself if you want to."

Dave decided that he'd like to visit Sapphire to see how she was doing. "I'll stop by later this afternoon," he said.

*   *   *

"So that clears up all those mysteries," said Neil, when he'd finished explaining to Helen the news about Sapphire. It was after lunch and Helen had arrived for their walk with the dogs in the park. Neil had suggested they wait until after Dave Morris's visit.

"Sapphire is so intelligent," Helen said. "I'd love to see some of the things she can do for Kevin."

"Perhaps Dave will show us," said Emily, looking out the kitchen window. "I think that's him now."

Neil peered out and saw a white van coming up the driveway. On each of the doors was a red logo that showed a figure in a wheelchair with a dog beside them and the black letters CPI printed below.

They ran out to meet Dave. Jake was the first to reach him.

"Hello, you friendly fellow," said the tall, dark-haired young man who climbed out of the van. He bent down to pat the Border collie. Jake welcomed him with an exuberant lick on his face, dislodging Dave's glasses.

"Sorry about that," Neil apologized.

"That's OK." Dave grinned, straightening his spectacles. "He can probably smell all the other dogs on me." He stood up. "You must be Neil, and one of you . . ." — he looked at the two girls — ". . . must be Emily."

Emily nodded. "That's me, and this is our friend Helen."

"Mom and Dad would like to meet you, too," said

Neil, leading the way through the gate to the kennel. "They asked if you could stay for a cup of coffee after you see Sapphire."

"Sounds good." Dave smiled.

They reached the rescue center and Neil explained why Sapphire hadn't been put with the regular boarders. "We were already overbooked when she came in on Sunday."

"Just as well," put in Helen, "because she and Trick have become great friends."

"Who's Trick?" Dave asked.

"The most gorgeous puppy you've ever seen in your life," Helen told him enthusiastically.

"I've seen a lot of gorgeous pups in my life," Dave warned her with a grin. "It would be hard to decide if one was more gorgeous than the rest."

"Oh, but Trick definitely is," Helen insisted.

They came to pen number four, and Sapphire recognized Dave immediately. She jumped up and expertly opened the gate by pushing down on the latch with her front paws. Then she bounded eagerly out of her pen.

"That's really smart of her," Emily declared.

"Actually, it's one of the first things they learn," said Dave proudly as he greeted the poodle with a warm hug. "She could keep you entertained for hours with all the things she can do. Sapphire just *loves* her work."

"That's probably why she couldn't resist doing the laundry," Neil joked.

"Hey, look!" Helen said suddenly. "Sapphire's not the only one who can open gates."

As if not wanting to be outdone by his neighbor, Trick was also letting himself out to join them. Unlike Sapphire, he wasn't tall enough to reach the gate fastening. But he had found a way around the problem — a bucket that had been left in his pen. Wobbling slightly, the determined puppy climbed on top of the upturned pail and nudged at the latch with his nose until the gate swung open. Within seconds he, too, was outside his pen, wagging his whole body with delight.

"You're a smarty, too," Helen told him proudly. She scooped Trick up in her arms and hugged him.

"I see what you mean," said Dave. "He's not just a handsome face. I wonder what else he can do?" He put his face close to Trick and the puppy sniffed Dave's nose, then squirmed to be put down.

Helen crouched down and put him on the floor. "He seems to be very good at retrieving," she said.

"And eating!" Emily laughed as Trick sucked up a tiny piece of dog biscuit.

"Typical of his breed," Dave commented. He turned to Neil. "Is he a stray?"

Neil nodded. "Yes. No one's come to claim him — even though we've advertised everywhere."

"Hmm. I wonder . . ." said Dave, watching Trick closely. He crouched down and clapped his hands together. "Come here, Trick," he called softly.

The pup looked across to Dave, then ran over to him, wriggling his soft body enthusiastically.

"You *are* a good boy," Dave praised him. "But let's see just *how* good you are." He looked up at Neil. "Is there somewhere I can take him on his own to do some basic tests?"

Before Neil could answer, Helen asked excitedly, "Do you think he could be an assistance dog like Sapphire?"

Dave laughed. "Hold your horses. It's way too early to be able to say that." He stroked Trick gently. "Canine Partners for Independence is always on the lookout for puppies that show promise. But having said that, I must also warn you that we don't often take strays and usually choose puppies when they're a bit younger than Trick — around six or seven weeks. Still, there's an exception to every rule."

"You can go into Red's Barn," Neil offered. "It's quiet in there."

Dave went to the van to fetch his bag.

"I'll get the camera," Emily said. "This will be something really interesting to put on the web site."

"Good idea," said Neil. He popped Sapphire back into her pen and told her to stay. Then he and Helen took Trick over to the barn.

"Wouldn't it be great if he could become an assistance dog like Sapphire?" said Helen. "I really, really hope he passes the tests."

Neil nodded, but he realized they shouldn't be too hopeful just yet. In order to do the kind of work expected of assistance dogs, a puppy needed to be really exceptional. On the surface, Trick seemed ideal, but who knew what Dave's tests would reveal? "Let's just keep our fingers crossed," he said cautiously.

CHAPTER NINE

"**W**ould you three mind keeping out of sight while I do the tests?" Dave asked when he came into the barn. "I need to see how Trick behaves with an unfamiliar person. His reactions to the tests may be different if he's with people he knows."

"Is it OK if we hide behind those straw bales?" Neil asked.

"That should be fine," said Dave. "Just as long as he can't hear or see you."

While Dave distracted the puppy, Neil, Emily, and Helen crept away quietly. When he realized they had gone, Trick looked around to see where they were. He sniffed the ground, picking up their scent, and started to head in their direction. But when Dave clapped his hands, he spun around and trotted back to him.

Dave patted Trick for a few moments, then rolled him over onto his back and gently held him down. Trick lay happily on the ground, gazing up at Dave and licking his hands with his soft, pink tongue.

"That's a good, confident boy," said Dave, picking him up and cuddling him close. "No struggling, nipping, or panicking." He put Trick back on the floor and made a note on a record card. Then he took out a squeaky toy and squeezed it.

Trick was fascinated by the noise. He sniffed the rubber toy in Dave's outstretched hand, then dabbed at it with his paw, trying to figure out where the noise had come from. Dave tossed it onto the ground and Trick scampered after it, landing on it with his front paws and making it squeak again.

While Trick was preoccupied with the toy, Dave took out a small personal alarm that he set off behind the puppy. Instantly alert, Trick looked around to see where the earsplitting screech was coming from. He noticed the alarm on the ground and trotted confidently over to investigate it.

"Great!" breathed Neil. "He's not afraid of loud noises."

There were two more tests. Dave checked Trick's reaction to a very strange prop — a pull-along plastic duck that clattered harshly and flapped its wings as it was tugged along. Trick showed no fear of the strange creature. He bounced inquisitively over to it and then, flopping down on his tummy, crawled along next to it as it moved forward.

"That's great, Trick," Dave murmured, grinning in the direction of the straw bales. "A lot of pups would try to attack it — if they're even brave enough to go near it," he explained for the benefit of his hidden audience.

For the final test, Dave dropped a metal teaspoon on the ground. Trick glanced at it, then looked back up at Dave and wagged his tail. Dave pointed to the spoon and held out his hand. "Come here, Trick," he said encouragingly.

Trick put his head to one side and furrowed his brow.

"Oh no!" gasped Helen in dismay. "He's not going to do it."

"Most dogs don't like picking up metal things," Emily whispered to her.

"What's this, Trick?" said Dave, squatting down and flicking the spoon with his fingers.

Trick gave a short bark but stayed sitting in front of Dave.

"Let's try this," said Dave, tapping the spoon a few times on the ground and wiggling it around in front of Trick.

Intrigued now, Trick stood up and circled the spoon. Then Dave threw it a short way ahead of him. Trick trotted after it.

"*Please* pick it up this time," Helen begged quietly. She clenched her hands tightly.

Trick sniffed the spoon, then looked back over his shoulder at Dave. The young man stood solemnly watching him, still holding out his hand.

Neil held his breath. What if Trick refused to pick it up? Would that count badly against him?

Suddenly, Trick seemed to realize what was wanted. Pouncing playfully onto the spoon, he gripped it between his front paws, then picked it up in his mouth.

Neil felt like cheering, but he managed to keep silent while Trick returned to Dave with the handle of the spoon sticking out of his mouth.

Emily laughed under her breath. "It looks like he's sucking a lollipop."

Dave took the spoon from Trick and rewarded him with a dog biscuit he'd taken out of his pocket. He

made another note on the record card. Then he called out, "That'll do for now. You three can come out."

"Did he pass?" Helen asked eagerly as they went over to Dave. She crouched down and hugged Trick, her face glowing with pride.

"Well, it's a start," said Dave. He bent down and stroked Trick. "He did very well on these tests. He's calm, gentle, and eager to please, and he shows initiative. But before we can go any further, he'll need to be checked thoroughly by a vet to ensure that he has no health problems — especially since we don't know anything about his background."

"Mike Turner can do that," Neil offered quickly. "He looks after all the dogs here."

"OK," said Dave. "Assuming he receives the all-clear from your vet, we need to make sure he can mix with other dogs and people. The best thing would be for him to come to a puppy class."

"What kind of puppy class?" Emily asked.

"We run weekly classes for puppies who are chosen to be assistance dogs," Dave explained. "If you like, you can bring Trick to the class in Padsham next week. A new group is starting. You'll be able to meet all the puppies and their puppy parents."

"Puppy parents?" Helen echoed. "Are those the disabled people?"

"No. A puppy isn't matched with an owner until it's finished all its training. And that takes at least fifteen months," Dave told them. He began to put the teaspoon and the toys back into his duffel bag. "You see, for the first twelve months, a CPI pup lives with a puppy-walking family. They attend classes every week for the puppy to be socialized and trained in a range of tasks. At the end of a year, the dog leaves its family and starts advanced training."

"It must be hard for people to have to give up a puppy they've looked after for a year," said Neil, thinking of how heartbroken he'd be if he couldn't keep Jake anymore.

"Yes, it's never very easy," Dave agreed. "But the rewarding part is knowing that the dog and the disabled person can do great things together. By the time a CPI dog goes to its special person, it knows one hundred different commands." He put the pull-along duck away and was closing the zipper on the bag when Trick jumped forward and began sniffing around, looking for the toy. "It's not yours," Dave told the pup, gently pushing him away.

But Trick persisted. He wanted to find the duck again. He leaned forward and inspected the bag as if looking for a way in. Then, to everyone's surprise, he gripped the tiny metal tongue of the zipper between his front teeth and pulled gently. The zipper slid open. Trick quickly pushed his head inside the bag and came out seconds later with the duck in his mouth.

Neil stifled a laugh. As far as he was concerned this was really smart behavior, but perhaps Trick had gone too far. Would Dave think he was being naughty? He glanced anxiously at Dave, who was standing with his arms folded — and a big grin on his face.

"What was I saying earlier about him showing *some* initiative?" Dave laughed. "He's a *master* at solving problems!" He kneeled down. "Give it to me," he said to Trick, holding out his hand.

Trick released the duck into Dave's hand, then sat in front of him with an expectant look on his face.

"Oops!" Dave chuckled, groping around in his pocket. "I forgot about the reward." He found a dog biscuit and gave it to Trick. "But you didn't, did you, boy?"

The following Wednesday afternoon, Bob dropped Neil, Emily, Helen, and Trick at the training center. It was in a single-story unit on a quiet industrial estate just outside Padsham.

Neil's first impression when they went inside was of a stage set that was a cross between a main street and the inside of a house. The walls were painted with such different scenes as shop fronts and fruit stalls, and lined with training props. There were washing machines, dryers, a telephone, shelves and drawers, and a pedestrian crossing.

From his vantage point in Helen's arms, Trick looked around, a bright expression on his face. He seemed very interested in his new surroundings — and in the seven other puppies romping about. Helen put him on the floor and he trotted confidently over to the others, greeting them with a friendly sniff and a lick. There were two golden retrievers, three Labradors — two black and one yellow — and two white Standard poodles.

"And you must be Trick," said a short, blond-haired woman, bending down and patting him. Trick licked her hand, then flopped down on his back while she tickled his tummy.

The woman looked up at Neil, Emily, and Helen, and introduced herself. "I'm Sandra, one of the trainers. Dave told me all about you three and this lovely little guy." She smiled down at Trick, who had spied a small blue-and-white plastic box that was hanging from a cord around her neck. He flipped over and stretched up toward the interesting-looking article.

"No, Trick," said Sandra, leaning back out of his reach. "This isn't a toy. It's a clicker, and you're going to find out all about it soon enough."

The class started with the puppies being weighed, and then they were introduced to the clicker.

"Clicker training is a positive way of teaching animals," Sandra explained. She held up her clicker and pressed it with her thumb. It made a loud, metallic click. Most of the puppies pricked up their ears and looked around to see where the noise had come from.

"I'll use one puppy to show you how the clicker works," said Sandra. Her eyes settled on Trick. "Trick can be my model, since he doesn't have a puppy parent yet."

Helen took Trick over to Sandra, then went back to Neil and Emily, who were standing at one side of the room. Trick watched Helen walk away, but quickly transferred his attention to Sandra as soon as she started talking again.

"We follow the sound of the clicker with tiny pieces of food," Sandra told them. "Like this." She bent down and held the clicker in front of Trick. He looked at it as Sandra clicked and, at the same time, gave him a small dog treat.

"Now you all do the same," Sandra instructed, looking around the rest of the class.

The other puppy parents practiced for a few minutes until all their dogs were well acquainted with the clicker. Soon, the sound of the click was enough to make all the tails — black, white, and golden — wag wildly in anticipation of a treat.

"OK," said Sandra. "Now that they have learned to link the noise to the treat, they will try to get you to click again." She looked down at Trick, who was gazing at her in the hope that she would click and treat him again.

"He's really sold on her!" Emily chuckled.

"Yes, it just shows what a sniff of food can do," Neil agreed.

Sandra went on. "Once he's figured out the behavior, then we teach him what the actual command is. Let me show you." She sat down in front of Trick. "We'll start with purse-touching. It's a very important part of early training for our puppies, because it gets them ready to start bringing things to us."

Sandra held a small purse in front of Trick and waited while Trick stared at her, expecting her to make the clicking noise again. But he soon became impatient and sniffed at the purse. Instantly, Sandra clicked and treated him. Then she waited again with the purse still in her hand.

"I bet he'll do it again really quickly," Helen whispered.

It took only few more attempts before Trick had figured out what was expected of him. Soon, Sandra introduced the word *purse*, and Trick knew that when he heard it, he had to touch the purse with his nose.

"That's so cool!" Neil exclaimed to Emily and Helen. He already knew that dogs were quick learners, but this was something else altogether!

A sudden thud at the back of the room made everyone turn around. One of the black Labradors had knocked a box of props off a table. The objects spilled out onto the floor and the puppy began to rummage through them. The puppy parent, a young woman with curly dark hair, hurried over and was about to pull him away when Sandra quickly called out, "Hold on, Deborah!"

The woman looked up, letting go of the puppy's collar.

"It's just that we don't deal with naughtiness in

the usual way," Sandra explained. "We never actually punish our dogs — instead, we show them what we do want, and reward them."

She beckoned to Helen and asked her to hold Trick while she dealt with the Labrador. "The best thing in this type of situation is to call him back to you and reward him for coming." She held up a squeaky toy and called, "Carling!"

The puppy pricked up his ears.

"Carling," Sandra repeated, crouching down and showing him the toy.

This time, Carling went bounding over to her, and Sandra clicked and treated him the moment he arrived. "He'll forget all about the things on the floor," she told his puppy parent, "now that he realizes it's more fun to be with me."

In the next hour, most of the puppies learned to touch the purse with their paws or noses. They also practiced commands for lying down, rolling over, and "shaking hands."

One of the poodles seemed more interested in investigating his neighbor than shaking hands. "I'll help you out," said Sandra to the puppy parent. She handed Helen a clicker. "Would you mind practicing with Trick for me?" she asked.

Helen didn't need to reply. Her broad smile said everything as she took the clicker from Sandra.

From the sidelines, Neil and Emily watched Helen give Trick the command to "shake hands." At once, the little golden dog held up his front paw. Helen took the paw, clicked, and fed him a treat.

"They're a great team!" said Neil admiringly.

When the class ended, Dave Morris came over to speak to Sandra. He had been watching Trick's progress from the window of his office at the far end of the room.

Neil, Emily, and Helen clustered around them, anxious to hear Dave's verdict on the puppy.

"He's a fast learner, isn't he?" Sandra said to Dave. "I think he shows real promise."

Helen couldn't contain her delight. "That's awesome!" she burst out.

Dave smiled and bent down to pat the little dog. "Well, Trick, you've certainly lived up to all our expectations," he said. Then he looked up at Sandra. "How do you feel about one more pupil in your class?" he asked.

CHAPTER TEN

Thrilled, Neil picked up Trick. The tired puppy nuzzled against his neck affectionately. Neil felt a moment's regret. It was really exciting that Trick was about to start a career as an assistance dog, but that meant Neil and the others would have to hand him over to his puppy parent.

"Do you have anyone lined up to be his puppy parent?" Neil asked Dave.

"No one in particular yet," Dave replied. "But now that we've decided to take Trick on board, I'll start going through the names of applicants in my file."

For a second, Neil thought that he would volunteer for the job, but he quickly realized it just wouldn't be practical. He had his own dog to take care of. *And train!* he told himself wryly, his mind flashing back to his attempts to teach Jake to retrieve the bowl in Red's Barn.

"You probably have lots of people who want to take a puppy," Helen said to Dave.

Dave nodded. "We try to make sure we select the most suitable people. But it's not always as easy as it seems. The family needs to be totally committed." He turned and gestured to the puppy parents, who were getting ready to leave. "For the next twelve months they're going to be pretty tied up. They'll have to bring their puppies to class every week — as well as take them out with them as much as possible."

"That doesn't sound too bad!" Neil grinned.

"But that's not all," Dave went on. "At the end of the year, just when they're all madly in love with their dogs and really proud of them, they have to give them up."

"That must be the hardest part," said Helen. She looked across at the puppy parents. "They must all be very dedicated."

Dave nodded. "They are. So you see, it's quite a tall order to care for one of our pups — not something you would take on lightly." He looked at Trick, who was now fast asleep in Neil's arms. "But we'll find him a good home, you can be sure of that. In the meantime," he said to Neil and Emily, "I'll arrange with your parents to take him home with me so that prospective people can come around to meet him."

Emily had been listening quietly to Dave, and as he

finished, a mysterious smile spread across her face. "I think I know the *perfect* home for him," she said.

"You do?" Dave asked, looking at her in surprise.

Neil glanced at his sister. Was she about to suggest herself?

"With Helen and her family," Emily announced. "She's crazy about Trick. I bet she'd look after him expertly — wouldn't you, Helen?"

Helen's eyes shone. "I definitely would. And I'd do everything you've just told us."

"Yes, but what about when he has to go on to advanced training?" Dave reminded her. "You might be too attached to him by then," he warned.

"But that's just the thing," Neil put in excitedly, as he realized just how much sense Emily's suggestion made. "You see, Helen and her parents are only in Compton for a year. By the time Trick is ready to leave, they'll be leaving, too."

But Dave wasn't convinced. "I know you're fond of Trick," he said to Helen. "But as I've already explained, that's not the only issue. It's a demanding job."

"I know — and I'm sure I can do it," Helen said earnestly.

"Yes, but you're at school all day," Dave pointed out. "And what about your parents? They might object to having a young dog in the house."

"They won't," Helen reassured him. "And Mom's at home all day, so he'd never be on his own. And when I'm not at school, I'll spend all my time with him!"

Dave didn't answer for a while. He stood with his chin cupped in one hand, looking at Helen thoughtfully.

Neil felt as if he would burst with suspense.

At last Dave cleared his throat. "Well, I'm not going to give you any false hope," he said honestly. "We'll have to check with your parents to see if they agree to the idea. Then we'll need to visit your home to make sure it's suitable."

Helen beamed. "It'll all be just fine," she said confidently. Then she put her face close to the sleeping puppy in Neil's arms and whispered, "You're coming to live with me, Trick."

*   *   *

Two days later, Neil and Emily were updating the King Street Kennels' web site when the phone rang. Neil picked it up.

"Neil!" exclaimed Helen's excited voice. "Guess what?"

Neil swallowed. "You mean —"

"Yes!" Helen burst out. "CPI have accepted us. We're Trick's puppy parents."

In the background, Neil could hear another sound — an enthusiastic sniffing. "Is that Trick I hear now?" he asked.

Helen laughed. "Yes. He's right here. Dave just brought him over. I think Trick wants to tell you the good news himself!"

Neil whistled softly into the phone and Trick responded with a cheerful yap.

Then Helen came back on the line and said, "There's one more thing."

"What's that?" Neil asked.

"Dave told us we need to appoint a foster family, in case we have to go away and can't take Trick with us," Helen told him. "Like with Sapphire and Mrs. Herson."

Neil guessed what Helen's next question would be. "And you want us to be that family?"

"Will you?" asked Helen.

Neil needed no persuading. "Of course," he said. "When are you going away?"

"Well, we haven't planned our vacation yet," Helen said. "But don't worry, because you're still going to be seeing lots of Trick. You can help me with his training if you like."

As soon as Neil put the phone down, he filled Emily in on Trick's new home.

Emily beamed. "Trick's turned into a real treat for Helen after all!" she said.

"Now remember, Jake, the *dish*," said Neil, showing the Border collie the bowl before putting it in the pile with all the other items. "You have to pick up the *dish* — not the other things."

It was Saturday afternoon and Neil was in Red's Barn with Jake. "I don't want the Frisbee or the dumbbell," he repeated as he led Jake to the back of the barn. "I want the dish." He turned and made Jake sit beside him, then, in a firm voice, he said, "Fetch the dish, Jake."

Eagerly, the black-and-white collie set off, his nose to the ground and his tail sticking straight out behind him. Neil waited with his arms crossed.

Jake reached the objects and, without even pausing, ran straight past them.

"No!" Neil shouted in exasperation as Jake shot out the door. He ran after him. "Jake!" he called. "Come here, boy."

But Jake was intent on something far more interesting. A red car had pulled into the driveway and the collie was bounding across the courtyard to greet the visitor.

That must be Kevin, Neil thought as he ran to catch up with Jake.

Kevin Dunbar had phoned earlier to say he would be picking up Sapphire that afternoon. Neil was looking forward to meeting him. He opened the gate that led to the driveway. Jake squirmed through and ran to the driver's door, his tail wagging happily.

Neil watched as Kevin lifted out the top part of a wheelchair and unfolded the compact frame before clipping on the wheels, which had been stowed on the floor in front of the passenger seat. Then the blond-haired young man slid out of the car and into the chair.

Fascinated by the strange new object, Jake planted himself solidly in front of it and proceeded to give the chair a thorough sniff. Kevin waited patiently and smiled at the excited dog.

"Sorry about that," Neil said, taking Jake's collar and pulling him away.

"That's OK," said Kevin. "I'm used to attracting attention."

Neil then introduced himself and Jake.

"He's a beautiful dog," Kevin said sincerely, patting the Border collie, who was still stretching forward to sniff at the wheels on the chair.

"He's the best dog in the world," Neil declared proudly. "Well, one of them. Sapphire's pretty amazing, too."

Kevin laughed. "The way I look at it is this: There is only one dog for me in the world, and that's Sapphire!" He bent over and ruffled Jake's fur. "But I'm sure this guy would come a close second."

Just then, the back door opened and Carole, Emily, and Sarah trooped out of the house to meet Kevin. Bob wasn't at home because he was taking one of the boarders back to its owner.

Emily handed Sapphire's papers to Kevin, and Sarah presented him with a drawing of the poodle unloading laundry from the dryer.

Kevin admired the colorful picture. "That's a good likeness," he said, smiling at Sarah. "And I'm glad to see Sapphire's been making herself useful!"

"She's been more than useful!" Carole laughed as they went across to the rescue center. "She's provided us with lots of entertainment."

"Mmm. She can be quite a clown, given the chance," Kevin agreed.

As he opened the door to the rescue center, Neil saw that Sapphire had heard Kevin coming across the yard. She was already out of her pen and waiting for him. Neil stood back and let Kevin go in first.

With a delighted whine, Sapphire jumped up and rested her front paws gently on Kevin's lap.

Kevin was just as pleased to see her. "I've really missed you," he said, hugging her closely to his chest and burying his face in her woolly coat.

Sapphire glanced over her shoulder at Neil, then began to lick Kevin's face as if to say, "This is *my* person."

Neil felt a lump in his throat. All the time that Sapphire had been at King Street Kennels, she had been calm and perfectly behaved, but she hadn't shown any real affection for any of them. Now she was smiling all over, wagging every inch of her body and whining with pleasure at being reunited with her owner.

Neil looked down at Jake, who was watching Sapphire intently. Jake suddenly spun around and gazed up at Neil with an expression that seemed to say, "And you're *my* person!" Neil grinned and reached down to stroke his ears.

"OK, Sapphire," said Kevin. "Time to go — we've got some shopping to do."

Sapphire jumped down as Kevin swung his wheelchair around and began to wheel himself back out into the courtyard. The poodle trotted beside him as if she was glued to the wheel.

"Does she help you with the shopping?" Sarah asked. She walked out next to Kevin, her hand resting lightly on one of the armrests.

"Yes. She takes items off the shelves and puts them in the basket for me," Kevin replied "She even knows how to put my bank card into the slot in an ATM machine and take out the money for me!"

"That's amazing!" said Emily. "Did you teach her that?"

"Actually, no. She taught herself when she saw me struggling to reach with the card one day," Kevin told her. "Sapphire always seems to know when I need help."

As he neared the car, Kevin's wheelchair hit a bump on the ground. The jolt made the folder containing Sapphire's documents slide off Kevin's lap. As it landed, it fell open and the papers spilled out. Emily darted forward, but Sapphire beat her to it and began carefully gathering the papers in her mouth.

When she had completed her task, Sapphire noticed that Kevin's right foot had slid off the footrest. She took it gently in her mouth and eased it back into place, then returned to Kevin's side as they moved off once more.

Neil swallowed hard. He quickly focused his attention on Jake. "Did you see that, boy?" he said with a grin. "Do you think you can learn to be half as helpful as Sapphire?"

Jake barked at him. "I'll try," he seemed to say.

"The main thing is to keep encouraging him," Kevin said. "If your dog wants to please you, you're halfway there."

They came to the gate and Kevin took a check out of his pocket and handed it to Carole to pay for Sapphire's stay. "Thanks so much for taking such good care of her," he said.

"It was our pleasure," Carole told him. Then, she said good-bye and headed back to the house.

Sarah gave Sapphire one last pat. "I'm going to teach Fudge to do lots of things, too," she said, and ran after Carole to begin training her long-suffering hamster.

"This I've got to see." Emily laughed, following her inside.

Sapphire pushed the gate open for Kevin, then nudged open the car door. She jumped onto the backseat and watched attentively as Kevin heaved himself out of his chair and into the driver's seat.

Kevin unclipped the wheels and put them on the floor, then folded up the frame of the wheelchair and pulled it across his lap onto the seat next to him. "Keep in touch!" he said to Neil as he turned the key in the ignition. "Dave tells me you've supplied him with a great little pup."

As Neil watched them drive away, he thought about what Kevin had said about training Jake. *I know Jake wants to please me,* he told himself. *So all he really needs is more encouragement.* He turned to go indoors. "Lunchtime, Jake," he said, patting his thigh.

But Jake had other ideas. Without a backward glance, he bounded away, heading straight for Red's Barn.

"Now what?" Neil protested, going after him.

But before Neil had gone very far, Jake came

hurtling out of the barn again — with a bulky silver object in his mouth.

Neil could hardly believe his eyes. It was the dish! Jake was bringing it to him.

"You amazing, awesome, wonderful dog!" Neil cried, taking the dish from Jake and burying his face in the collie's silky black-and-white coat. "No matter what other dogs can do, you're the only one in the world for me!"